The Rich Man and the Parrot

Retold by **Suzan Nadimi**

Illustrated by **Ande Cook**

ALBERT WHITMAN & COMPANY, MORTON GROVE, ILLINOIS

To Michael, for his support.–S.N.

To "Bear."–A.C.

Library of Congress Cataloging-in-Publication Data

Nadimi, Suzan.
The rich man and the parrot / retold by Suzan Nadimi ; illustrated by Ande Cook.
p. cm.
Summary: In this retelling of a tale by Rumi, a parrot tricks a wealthy merchant into setting him free.
A retelling of a Persian folktale attributed to (Jalal al-Din) Rumi (1207-1273).
ISBN-13: 978-0-8075-5059-5 (hardcover)
[1. Parrots–Folklore. 2. Folklore–Iran.] I. Cook, Ande, ill. II. Title.
PZ8.1.N1413Ric 2007 398.2–dc22 [E] 2006025183

Text copyright © 2007 by Suzan Nadimi. Illustrations copyright © 2007 by Ande Cook.
Published in 2007 by Albert Whitman & Company, 6340 Oakton Street, Morton Grove, Illinois 60053-2723.
Published simultaneously in Canada by Fitzhenry & Whiteside, Markham, Ontario.
Printed in the United States of America.
10 9 8 7 6 5 4 3 2 1

The design is by Carol Gildar.

For more information about Albert Whitman & Company, visit our web site at www.albertwhitman.com

About Rumi

The story "The Rich Man and the Parrot" comes from the *Masnavi,* a work by the thirteenth-century Persian poet Mawlana Jalal ad-Din Rumi. Rumi was born in 1207 in the city of Balkh (then a part of Persia, now Afghanistan). His father, Bahauddin, was a great religious thinker with many followers. When Rumi was five years old his family left Balkh and spent several years traveling abroad. When Rumi was eighteen, he met Farid ad-Din Attar, one of Persia's greatest mystic poets. Attar immediately recognized Rumi's talent. Upon seeing him walking behind his father, he said, "Here comes the sea followed by an ocean." Attar gave Rumi one of his books, which had a deep impact on Rumi and later influenced his poetry. Eventually, Rumi took his father's place as the head of a religious school, practicing Sufism, a mystic tradition of Islam. Today, Rumi's work is read all around the world, and his words and wisdom inspire a diverse audience.

Once upon a time in Persia there lived a rich merchant whose mansion was filled with exquisite treasures. He had smooth silk from China, intricate jewelry from India, and colored glass from the West.

Of all the beautiful things he owned, however, the merchant loved a parrot from India the most.

For this was not an ordinary parrot, but a parrot that entertained the lonely merchant with old legends and tall tales.

The merchant had built for his parrot a garden
of tall sycamore trees, sweet-smelling jasmine bushes, and
rippling fountains of cool blue water. He took care of his
parrot's every wish—except for one.

"I am sorry," the merchant would say each time the parrot asked to be freed from his cage. "But you'll fly away from me sooner or later, as birds always do. And I can't bear to part with you."

One day the merchant told his parrot, "I'm traveling to India. Is there anything you want from your homeland? Tell me, and I will buy it."

"I do desire something, and you need not pay coins of gold for it," the parrot answered. "When you happen to pass by the jungle, give my greetings to my brothers. Tell them that I often think of the days when we flew free. And, please Master, bring me back their reply."

The merchant traveled to India and loaded his caravan with spices, jewels, and gold. On the last day of his stay, he visited the jungle, just as he had been asked. There he saw the beautiful parrots so much like his own bird.

"Dear parrots," he called out. "I bring you a message from your brother."

The parrots listened intently as the merchant delivered the message.
"My parrot would like an answer," the merchant said when he was done.
"Do you have one for him?"

None of the parrots spoke.

The merchant spoke louder. "Do you have
a message for your brother?"
Again, they did not reply.

The merchant thought that perhaps none of the parrots could talk the way his could. He was about to turn back when a parrot fell to the ground.

"Oh, no!" the merchant cried.
Soon another parrot fell. And then another and another . . .

until there were no more parrots perching on the branches. They all lay upon the jungle floor, lifeless and still.

"Angels of heaven assist me!" The merchant beat upon his head. "What will I tell my parrot?"

The merchant returned home with a heart as heavy as the bags of riches in his caravan.

"Greetings, Master," the parrot said. "How was your trip?"

The merchant told the parrot about the people he had met, the foods he had eaten, the sights he had seen.

Finally he said, "I went to see your brothers and delivered your message. Alas! They didn't reply."

"They didn't reply?" asked the parrot in surprise.

The merchant recounted how the parrots listened but never spoke; how they had all fallen to the ground, one after the other, stiff as rocks.

As soon as the merchant finished, *his* parrot
fell to the bottom of his cage, lifeless and still.

"The wrath of God is upon me!" the merchant sobbed. He flung open the cage door to cradle his parrot.

In an instant, the parrot was flying away.

"You're alive!" shouted the merchant
as he followed the parrot through the trees.
    "And free . . . thanks to my brothers'
reply!" said the parrot.
    "But they didn't say anything!"
panted the merchant.

"They replied not with words
but with deeds," said the parrot.
"My greeting was really a plea for help.

"When my brothers held their tongues, they told me that the sweetness of my tongue was holding me captive. And when they froze and fell to the earth, they showed me the way to freedom. I froze and fell, too, pretending to be dead.

"You opened my cage only when you thought I could no longer fly away."

"Stay with me!"
the merchant pleaded.

"I've always given you all
of your heart's desires."

"Except for the one that mattered the most," said the parrot . . .

and he flew home.